Oliver Anderson

and the

Assumption Bumption

by Daph Talley

illustrated by Bethany Dillard

ISBN: 978-0-578-84397-1

FIRST EDITION

This is for my Aunt Rita, because she always said I could do this.

For my family and friends who have encouraged and helped me.

But mostly for my children and Freddie Mercury.

Oh yeah, and you too Zane.

-Daph

This is for my mom and dad who always encouraged my talents.

Also, for my husband and children who support all my crazy dreams.

-Bethany

Oliver Anderson lived on a hill with his father, his mother, and his pet penguin Phil.

I should mention
the season,
it was summer you see,
they had long sunny
days
that were fun
filled and
free.

They'd put Phil on his harness ('cause hey, safety first),

then walk to the park at Hastings and Hurst.

They would visit with friends and go down the big slide,
then take turns on the see-saw (it was Phil's favorite ride).

Each day was quite pleasant, each day was the best 'til along came Mack Harper, the neighborhood pest.

Mack was a bald kid with muddy brown eyes
and according to rumors,

ate tree frogs
and flies!

He had a big bump right on his left shoulder;

it started out small

then grew

to a **boulder**!

What was that thing? From where did it come?
"Well don't ask old Mack 'cause he's stupid and dumb!"

"He doesn't know much, only knows how to hit,

and jump up and down
in occasional fits."

"Ollie," said Syd, "look, Mack's coming here!
Let's get Phil and go!" Her voice trembled with fear.

But Oliver Anderson was not one to run; it was summer, by golly, and he meant to have fun.

He would not run away nor shiver nor shake; he would make his face brave, even if it were fake.

Syd pulled Phil closer, his harness held tight. Mack's face was cloudy like he wanted to fight.

This seemed pretty scary, this looked really bad.

Someone get help!

Call a mom or a dad!

But no help
could be had; mom and dad
were at work. Our friends were
alone to deal with
this jerk.

He reached out a hand; he was grabbing for Phil.
The penguin stepped backwards and took quite a spill.

He had tripped on a rock,
fell back with a thump and plopped down
quite hard on his
chubby black rump!

If truth should be told, Phil was okay, but
Oliver Anderson didn't see it that way.

His fear
disappeared and
he pushed Mack
quite hard;

this kind of
anger caught
him off guard.

He was usually friendly, full of good will,
but he loved his dear penguin,
you **DO NOT** mess with Phil.

With no warning at all, Mack started to cry; his big, stubby fingers wiped at his eyes.

Our friends were confused by this big, crying grump and the obvious growth of his weird looking bump.

"Why did you push me?" Mack asked through his tears, and
instead of anger,
he showed

worry

and

fear.

Well," sputtered Ollie, "You came after Phil. What should I do? Just be quiet and still?

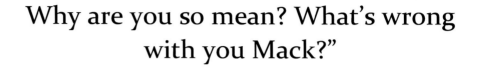

Why are you so mean? What's wrong with you Mack?"

The anguished response was, "I didn't attack."

"I once had a penguin, he was loyal and brave. He is no longer with me, I miss my friend Dave.

I saw you with Phil and I felt very sad. I thought if I held him, I might not feel bad."

Ollie and Syd were left without words. What was the meaning of what they'd just heard?

The thought of old Mack with a heart that could feel,

didn't make sense; didn't seem real.

The friends felt so sad for the pain that Mack bore.

Syd's voice was quiet, "Please Mack, tell us more."

Well," Mack began wiping his tears, "Dave was my friend for so many years.

We were always together, never apart and when he went away that loss hurt my heart."

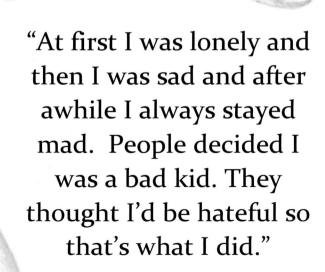

"At first I was lonely and then I was sad and after awhile I always stayed mad. People decided I was a bad kid. They thought I'd be hateful so that's what I did."

They were so busy making assumptions, and those negative
thoughts caused the growth of this Bumption.

But I'm tired of this; I want it to end.
I'm not a bad person. I just miss my friend."

Ollie's heart softened and he knew Syd's did too, it became very clear just what they should do.

Ollie said, "Mack, it's quite clear to see; you don't need a friend, but instead you need three."

Phil tugged on his harness and broke free from Syd and can you just guess the next thing that he did?

If you guessed he hugged Mack, then my friend you guessed right! He leapt into his arms and squeezed him so tight!

Mack was surprised and he felt himself smile. He hadn't felt so much joy in awhile.

Not wanting to wait one second more, Ollie and Syd turned the huggers to four.

And what happened next? Well, what do you think?
The bump on Mack's shoulder just started to shrink!

The more he felt loved,

the less he felt frightened.

His troubles got smaller!

His burden was lightened!

Ollie stepped back with Phil now in his arms. He quietly said, "Mack **WE'VE** done **YOU** some harm. Our words have been careless. We've been quick to judge. We formed our opinions and just wouldn't budge."

The new found friends talked;
the trouble had passed.
Mack found a place to belong at
long last.

He thought about Dave and his throat had a lump,
but despite the new tears, away went that bump.

And with each passing day, no matter the weather, the sun seemed to shine when the four were together.

The End

Questions for the reader:

- Do you have a best friend? What is their name? (It's okay if you don't; not everyone does…or you can have more than one!)

- Do you have chores? Which do you like the best? Which do you like the least?

- Do you have or want a pet? What kind of pet?

- What would "the best day" look like to you? Who would be with you? What would you do?

- Have you ever been afraid of another person (kid or adult). What did you do? Did you tell a trusted grown up

- Have you ever become friends with someone that you didn't like so much at first?

- How do you handle it when you don't like how someone is behaving?

- Do you have some friends who call someone names? What's a better thing to do?

- Have you ever wanted to hit or push someone? What's a better thing to do?

- Do you think it's important to understand that sometimes we make choices that we don't realize are bad (like being mean to someone who is mean to us) and apologize?

- Mack seemed mad, but it turned out that he was very sad. Have you ever felt or acted mad when you were just really sad?

- Is there anyone that you'd like to be friends with? How can you let them know you'd like to be friends?

About the Author

Daph Talley is a Chef and Mom who has loved writing all her life. She has a soft spot for children's books, as many of her best childhood memories have to do with reading.

Daph loves overseas travel and gets many of her ideas from experiences she has in England.

She lives in Oklahoma with her 2 children and a couple of very naughty dogs.

About the Illustrator

Bethany Dillard is a full-time high school teacher, respiratory therapist, dance teacher, and artist.

Bethany has been drawing and painting since she could pick up a pencil and brush. Her favorite is painting murals and now creating illustrations.

She lives in Oklahoma with her husband, 3 children, 1 dog, and 2 cats.

Made in the USA
Monee, IL
22 January 2022